THE CAVE

THE CAVE

BY ELIZABETH COATSWORTH

ILLUSTRATED BY ALLAN HOUSER

THE VIKING PRESS · NEW YORK

LITHOGRAPHED IN U. S. A. BY MURRAY PRINTING CO.

For Margaret Smith

with love

THE CAVE

The thing rushing toward him was the first train Jim Boy-Who-Loves-Sheep had ever seen. But he stood his ground and did not even glance up at his big brother Harvey Two-Crows standing beside him, his thumbs hooked in his belt. Jim's bright Navajo eyes never left the wonderful train, and because he was a maker of songs he was singing one now to himself:

> "Come on in beauty, great horse,
> Stamp your feet on the iron trail,
> Come on in beauty, great horse,
> Neighing you come,
> Stamping your feet you come,
> Breathing out smoke you come,
> Out of the east you come,
> In beauty you come,
> Great horse."

Even when the engine pounded, whistling, to the siding, Jim never moved.

He would have liked to watch the engine take on water at the tank, but just then a tall, dark-haired man, followed by two black and white sheep dogs, stopped to ask Harvey a question, and, catching Jim's eye, gave the boy a quick smile. He was almost as dark as an Indian, but he was not an Indian. When he went on, Harvey said that he was Fernando, the ranch sheep-herder, and that he came from a tribe called Basques who lived across the sea.

"He likes sheep almost as much as you do," Harvey said. "He's meeting a carload of specially fine ewes which the boss is expecting today to add to his flock. Soon they will all be leaving for the summer pasture in the mountains."

"How many will there be altogether?" Jim asked, always interested in hearing about sheep.

"About a thousand," Harvey said carelessly. He had worked on the Three H Ranch for a year and a thousand sheep were only a thousand sheep to him. But to Jim, who had taken care of his mother's sixty sheep and goats, a thousand sheep seemed the most wonderful

10

thing in all the world. He was not called Boy-Who-Loves-Sheep for nothing. Harvey had always liked horses and cattle better.

"Can't we watch the sheep unload?" Jim begged.

"I have to pick up some canned goods for the ranch," said Harvey. "You go on. When the ewes have been unloaded, you'll find me parked near the door of the freight office over there."

Jim nodded and hurried off. He had been visiting his brother at the ranch for only a day so far, but already he was used to seeing Harvey drive a big truck and to hearing him talk almost like a white man. When they were alone together they spoke in Navajo, but with others they talked in English, Harvey easily and Jim as well as he could.

Already the sheep were beginning to clatter down the ramp from one of the freight cars. The journey had frightened them. First they would not come at all. Then they came all at once, crowding and snorting, some trying to climb over the others in their fear. They were in danger of breaking their legs. The young black and white dog caught the excitement and began to bark and nip at them. That frightened them all the more.

Fernando and the old dog were trying to quiet things down when a red-faced man on a fine buckskin horse rode up, and threw the flock into a new panic.

"Stop that fool of a dog!" he shouted.

"He must be the boss of the ranch," Jim thought as he ran toward the sheep, which the horse and the shouting man had made more terrified than ever. Jim did not even know what he was doing. It was natural for him to help sheep. Now he moved among them, touching them with his hands. He sang to them, in Navajo:

> "Go quietly, my little ewes.
> The danger of the train is over.
> Go quietly, my little ewes,
> There are only friends here.
> To green pastures you are going,
> To long grass you are going,
> To the shadow of pine trees you are going,
> And cold water, clear and sweet.
> The coyotes shall not hurt you,
> The mountain lions shall not hurt you,
> You shall feed on nothing poisonous.
> Go quietly, my little ewes,
> Quietly."

14

The ewes did not understand the words of Jim's song, but they felt that the boy was a friend. The singing and the touch of his hands eased their fear. In a few minutes the flock was quiet, starting on the road for the ranch.

"Here I am," called Harvey from the truck as they passed by the freight office.

"I will stay with the sheep," answered Jim.

Fernando, on the other side of the flock, gave the boy a grateful glance. It was the last friendly look Jim was to have from Fernando for days to come.

15

The boss had followed, walking the buckskin, and now he called Jim over to where he sat watching everything.

"You're Harvey's kid brother, aren't you?" he asked. "I see you understand sheep. The ewes are soon going to summer pasture. If you will go with them, to help Fernando on the journey into the mountains, I'll let you take your choice of one of them and her lamb, too."

"My father and mother would not know where I was."

"Weren't you going to visit Harvey for a week or

16

two? You can be back on the reservation inside that time."

Jim didn't say yes and he didn't say no. This was a thing he would have to think about before he decided. The boss understood.

"We'll talk it over later," he said, and, loosening the buckskin's reins, he was off. Harvey followed slowly with the truck, and the sheep bunched and then started to run. But the dogs kept them on the road, and soon their fear again died down.

Fernando was a good sheepherder, quick of eye and careful, and the old dog knew just what to do. The young dog was showier, but he kept the sheep excited. Again and again Fernando called him back. The sheepherder paid no attention to Jim. It was as though the boy weren't there at all. Once when Jim asked him a question, he made no answer. It gave Jim a queer feeling. One moment Fernando was his friend, and the next he seemed more like an enemy.

But the sheep needed him. He sang to them, and talked to them and urged on the stragglers. They were all fine young sheep. To Jim they did not look ugly, even though they had recently been shorn for the summer and their necks were thin and all their joints showed. He sang:

> "Go quietly, my little ewes,
>   There are only friends here."

But to himself he added, "Fernando is not my friend now."

"What will you do, then?" Harvey asked.

The two brothers were sitting with their backs to a

cottonwood tree by the wash. The moon had just risen
over the mesa to the east and seemed to be looking for

something. Everything gleamed white except the yellow lamplighted windows of the ranch house, and one little fire by the corrals.

"How long is the journey?"

"It should take only four days—one day along the valley to Cedar Springs, one day in the lower foothills. The third day you go past the Canyon of the Dead."

"The Canyon of the Dead?" Jim repeated. "Surely no one goes there! Our uncle has told me all about it."

Long, long ago when his people were at war with the Apaches, the old men and women and children took refuge in a great cave in a hidden canyon while the young men were on the war path. From the top of the cliff only one narrow trail led to the cave. The Apaches did not find this path, or more likely they found it but knew that it could be easily defended, for they stayed on the mesa above the cave until all the Navajo people died of hunger and thirst rather than be taken prisoners. Their bones were still there, and it was a haunted place. It was not lucky even to speak its name, if it could be helped. No Navajo ever went near it.

The very thought of it made Jim feel cold.

"The way leads along the mesa above the canyon,"

said Harvey. "The people here know nothing about the cave, not even that it is there. And on the fourth day you come to the summer meadows where the grass is thick and there is plenty of water. And wild horses and deer."

"Then there are plenty of coyotes, too, and mountain lions."

"Of course," said Harvey. "Last year there was trouble. But Fernando has his gun. That is his problem. You have only to go with them for four days."

"Coming down I would be alone."

Harvey did not answer. A ranch hand was singing by the bunkhouse and he seemed to be listening to the song. Jim, too, sat for a long time, saying nothing more. He liked the idea of having a sheep and a lamb. In his mother's flock half a dozen of the ewes were his, but these ranch sheep were much finer than the Indian sheep. Still, it was not so much the thought of earning a sheep that attracted him. He was drawn by the idea of this great flock of almost a thousand animals, flowing upward like a slow great river from the parched valley into the green mountain pastures. He wanted to be with them, to serve them.

21

"Fernando no longer likes me," he said at last.

Harvey made no reply. Yet Jim knew that he had heard. Harvey's thinking went along with Jim's, strengthening it. They considered the Canyon of the Dead, Fernando's unfriendliness, the need of the sheep. When Jim finally said, "I will go," Harvey said, "Yes, you will go."

"When will it be?"

"The boss hasn't said. Tomorrow they will shear the last of the ranch sheep. When you go, you will take a blanket and a sheepskin to lie on. One of the burros will carry what you and Fernando need."

The night was so fine that the boys decided to sleep under the cottonwood tree. Late into the night Jim lay thinking of his mother and father and of his uncle who told him stories, and of Antelope, his little sister. He missed them, but it was good to be with Harvey again. If only he had been going into the mountains with Harvey instead of with Fernando!

On the next day the last of the sheep were sheared, and that night Jim slept in the bunkhouse, but long before dawn he heard through his dreams, "Wake up! Wake up! We're leaving!"

22

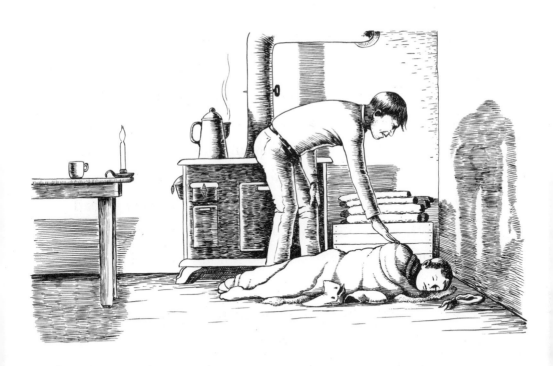

It was Fernando's voice in his ears. It was Fernando's hand that was shaking his shoulder, and there
was no friendliness in either of them.

Jim rolled over and got to his feet. A candle had
been lighted and the shadows in the bunkhouse were
long and dark. The other men were asleep, but Harvey
woke up and smiled at him. A smell of coffee came
from the stove.

Fernando was already gulping some down and

eating cold corn bread. "Hurry! We haven't got all day," he exclaimed.

Now Harvey was up and making a bundle of a blanket and sheepskin. "I put in some dried meat," he said in a low voice. "You may want it on the way back."

The coffee was hot and hard to swallow. Why did Jim's heart feel so heavy? He had been having bad dreams, and now evil spirits seemed to be moving among the shadows in the bunkhouse. He rubbed his eyes, hoping to wake up and shake off the heaviness that weighed him down. But it only grew worse. He followed Harvey to the door.

The stars were paling in the light of the coming morning. Only the morning star hung clear and golden in the east. Already the sheep were stirring. A murmur rose from the great pasture where they lay.

"It will be a good day," said Harvey, a dark figure, holding the bundle. "You will be back in a week, or maybe a day over, if the weather stays good."

"It is too early to take the sheep into the mountains!" said Jim. "I feel it, Harvey. It is too early."

Fernando crowded past them, also with a bundle. "Come along if you're coming," he said.

24

Jim tried again. "I don't like this day, Fernando."

The man gave a short laugh. "Who cares what you like?" he asked. "The grass here is giving out, and we have the boss's orders. He told me last night to get started at dawn."

"It is not a good day," Jim repeated, but no one had time to listen.

Even Harvey only said, "Help me load the burro. Don't worry. You've got nothing to do with it. What the boss says, goes."

Half an hour later the sheep were moving along the valley, feeding as they went. The dogs ran, one on each side, and Fernando and Jim followed with the pack burro. Jim carried an old tin can filled with pebbles, which he shook at any of the ewes lagging behind. The valley was filled with the sound of the sheep, and above them hung the yellow dust raised by their hoofs.

As the flock flowed slowly along, the rams in the home pasture baaed deeply in farewell, and the ewes answered. Lost lambs bleated for their mothers, and mothers replied, and now and then the young dog barked excitedly, or Fernando shouted an order.

It all seemed as it should seem, yet Jim felt that something was wrong. The ewes were uneasy. And the burro showed more than a burro's unwillingness to start off on a journey. The young dog was pleased and excited, but Jim thought that he saw an anxious look in the eyes of the old black and white collie.

Jim began to sing as he walked along:

> *"Make my path straight,*
> *For my heart is heavy.*
> *If there are dangers in the sky,*
> *Let them not come near the flock.*

26

If there are dangers from the earth,
Let them be turned away.
If the spirits are angry,
Let them be at peace.
Let the ewes walk in peace,
Let the lambs follow them in peace,
Let there be peace between us
Who guard the sheep from evil."

Usually when he sang his troubles left him, as if blown away on the wind, but today singing was of no help.

A mile from the ranch the boss overtook them to give the flock a last looking-over, and to say good-by to Fernando. "Someone will be up with more supplies in a couple of weeks. You'll be able to shoot what meat you need in that country. Well, so long, Fernando. I hope things go better this year."

"Boss," said Jim, coming up.

"Yes?"

"Boss, I—" Jim had made up his mind to say that after all he wouldn't go with the sheep. Something was wrong. He felt it. "Boss—"

28

"What is it, boy? Do you think I'm not paying you
enough? It's all right with me if you choose a ewe with
twin lambs. Do you hear, Fernando? He can take two
lambs if he likes."

"It isn't that—"

But the boss was impatient. He couldn't wait while
Jim tried to find words in which to explain this uneasy
feeling of his. And after all, Jim found that he couldn't
leave the sheep. If trouble was coming, they would need
him.

"All right, boss," he said.

The boss smiled. "Good," he said. "So long, both of you."

"Always he speaks of last year!" Fernando said angrily to himself. "Get going! Get going there!" he yelled to the sheep. "We have to make the springs by dark."

All day they moved through sage country with red mesas beside them. Sometimes they lost many minutes driving the sheep out of the way of one of the rare automobiles, each moving under a cloud of its own dust.

At noon the sheep rested and Fernando and Jim found a little shade beside a rock, with the dogs lying near them. Birds were singing their spring songs and everywhere there were desert flowers. Later on Jim saw a rattlesnake and stood quietly to let it pass, wondering what message it was taking to the gods.

He would have been happy in that great slow flow of the sheep, surrounded by the callings of the lambs and their mothers, if the sense of danger had not hung over him.

30

He looked at the sky. A hawk floated above him on motionless wings, but there seemed no danger there.

He watched the wind, but the golden cloud of dust raised by the moving flock scarcely stirred above their heads.

Last year the ewes had gone even earlier than this to pasture. Harvey had told him so. And yet the boy felt uneasy and he thought that the animals were uneasy, too.

And Fernando's silence troubled him. There are two silences; one is friendly and one is not. Fernando's silence was not friendly.

32

Even that first day Jim noticed the independent old ewe with the black lamb. She always moved on one side of the flock, and rested a little away from the others. She seemed glad to see Jim, not at all afraid of him, and willing to let him come up and pat the lamb.

"She must have been an orphan and brought up at the ranch," he thought. "She doesn't seem to know that the sheep are her people."

He called her Goes-Off-By-Herself.

They made the springs that evening and ate a silent meal. The moon came up in a cloudless night sky, paling the stars. Very early the two herders got out their

33

sheepskins and blankets, but there was little sleep for them. It was the burro who made the trouble, hee-hawing rustily. For five minutes on end she would bray;

then silence would come again. But just as they would be dropping off to sleep, the uproar would begin again.

All of a sudden Fernando's nerves gave way. Leaping to his feet, he caught up his sheepherder's staff and began to beat the burro. It seemed as if he couldn't stop.

Jim lay still for a while but at last he could put up with it no longer. He jumped to his feet and shook Fernando's shoulder. "That is enough," he said.

The man turned a face whitened by anger and the moonlight. He forgot the burro and whirled on Jim. For a moment the boy thought that the staff would next

come down on him, but Fernando stopped himself just in time.

"Go on back," Fernando said in a choked voice. "I don't need a boy to teach me my business, whatever the boss thinks. It wasn't my fault last year." And suddenly he stopped, as if he had said too much, turned about, and went back to his sheepskin and blanket.

Jim could not lie down again until his thoughts had become quiet. He was not angry with Fernando. Surely an evil spirit had entered into the herder. He needed a medicine man to bring him back to the path of beauty, but all that a boy could do was keep himself from becoming like Fernando.

Jim stood and looked up at the star people for a long time. Like the sun they, too, moved westward toward the sea where the Turquoise Woman lived in her turquoise-and-coral house. The smell of sheep and of sage came to him as he stood there. He felt the earth under his moccasins and was comforted by it. Spot, the old dog, came close beside him. He said nothing, but Jim heard his dog heart speaking: "I am here. I will help you all I can. Something is wrong, but we will make it right."

Some of the sheep were lying down and some stood quietly, almost invisible in the moonlight. It was their shadows that Jim saw, rather than the sheep. When he walked among them, they looked at him as he passed by with the dog.

"We are the sheep people. We give you our wool and mutton to eat. Take care of us," they said to him.

"I will take care of you," he answered without words.

Now beauty was returning to his heart. He saw that the moonlight was so bright that the mesa beyond the spring showed dull red and a few stalks of yucca blossoms growing far up in a crevice were as white as great candles.

When he circled back to his sheepskin, he came upon Goes-Off-By-Herself and the black lamb, lying away from the others in a little hollow.

"Don't you know that the coyotes are hungry?" Jim scolded her. "Go back to the flock." She tried to tell him something, but he knew only a few phrases of sheep talk and could not understand. She kept turning her head toward the far-away ranch, and perhaps he guessed her meaning.

"Something is wrong," he said. "We all feel it, but

we cannot go back. What is it we fear, you and I? See how bright the moon is in the moon carrier's arms! And it is not early in the season, even for sheep who have been sheared. I have heard the coyote people, but they are hunting far off. Perhaps everything is all right. The boss is a wise man, or how would he own so many sheep? And this man from across the sea has lived with sheep all his life. He sees nothing wrong."

The burro began to bray as Jim came near the campfire, and he went to talk with her as he had talked to the sheep. "Rest, Long-Ears. We have far to travel tomorrow and you will be tired as well as we." And

39

very soon, as if she understood him, the burro became silent.

The morning star, bright in the east, saw the flock once more on its way. Again the river of sheep rolled slowly along under a golden cloud. Their newly sheared whiteness deepened to the golden-red color of the earth. Once again the blue sky arched overhead, and the sun carrier's white horse proudly moved across the heavens. The trail on this second day rose, but not steeply. The ewes and lambs were fresh. They climbed easily, browsing and calling as they went. Only a few of the oldest sheep and the youngest lambs lagged behind and had to be hurried with shouts or the rattle of stones in Jim's tin can.

It was during the noon rest that for the first time danger struck. As Jim sat eating the noonday meal, a sudden increased feeling of uneasiness came over him, and with the food still in his hands he got up. From where he stood he could see most of the flock, standing or lying about in what shade they could find. Nothing seemed wrong.

But he was not satisfied. He walked back along the

home trail a little way, and suddenly a violent motion
caught his eye.

41

To one side, he saw Goes-Off-By-Herself, with her black lamb behind her, backed against a rock. The old ewe was standing, pawing the ground, and circling in front of her was a young coyote.

When the coyote shot forward toward the lamb, the ewe lowered her head and lunged at him with all the force of her narrow skull.

Jim was filled with admiration. He had never heard of a ewe who would make a stand against a coyote. A ram might, but not a ewe! Yelling and rattling his tin, he ran toward the group, and the coyote broke away and fled.

The lamb was untouched but the old sheep had deep cuts on her shoulders and neck where the killer's teeth had slashed.

"The best thing is to butcher her for meat," said Fernando, when he saw her. "She will not be strong enough for the trail."

But he gave way before Jim's indignation.

"See that she keeps up," Fernando said with a shrug. Then he added, "I admire courage, too. Here is the salve. Do what you can."

Goes-Off-By-Herself seemed to know that Jim was

42

trying to help her. Without protest, she let him handle her. She bore her wounds bravely like a warrior, he told her.

Often during the long afternoon he walked beside her, singing to keep up her heart.

> *"The meadows are above us*
> *Where the rainbows stand,*
> *There falls the warm rain,*
> *There the flowers blossom.*
> *The grass is green*
> *In the high meadows*
> *Where the rainbows stand."*

Goes-Off-By-Herself seemed to listen. That night she and the black lamb lay near the cooking fire, and the next day she was stronger.

Once again the air was clear and the sky was bright. The trail rose more steeply now, and there was more grass for the flock and the air was cooler.

But Jim's heart was heavy with dread. He knew that this was the day when they would pass the Canyon of the Dead with its haunted cave. Ghosts are always evil, his uncle had told him, even the ghosts of his own people. And ghosts who had died of hunger and thirst would be more terrible than others, he knew.

It was late in the afternoon when they came to the place. Jim could see below them a narrow canyon. The rock was white—almost like bones, he thought. Its whiteness seemed to him horrible, and he tried not to look at it. For perhaps two miles the trail led almost along the edge of the Canyon of the Dead, and all that time Jim was so frightened that he moved like a sleep-walker with staring eyes and his hands hanging at his sides.

44

Goes-Off-By-Herself seemed to crowd against his knees as if she too were afraid, and all the flock baaed and bleated anxiously, and the burro hung back and had to be hauled along by her halter.

Trying to see nothing, nevertheless Jim saw the trail that led off to the cave, and knew it for what it was, as if he had seen the ghosts walking along it.

> *"Be at rest, Ancestors.*
> *Be at rest, Old Ghosts.*
> *Be at rest, Terrible Ones.*
> *We do not mean to disturb your sleep.*
> *Let us pass by your house quickly.*
> *Be blind to us,*
> *Be deaf to us,*
> *Do not think of us,*
> *We shall soon be gone, Old Spirits."*

It seemed to Jim a long, long time before the canyon lay behind them. Nothing had stirred in the bone-colored depths. Not even an owl had cried, nor a messenger snake crossed their path. He felt safer now. The load of anxiety he had carried seemed lighter on his shoulders. Perhaps, after all, the only danger had been his fear of the canyon.

46

Fernando called a halt earlier than Jim could have
wished.

"Shall we not go on a little farther?" Jim asked.

"Why?"

"To be away from the canyon."

"What's wrong with the canyon?" Fernando de-
manded. "The sheep won't fall into it! We have a long,
hard day tomorrow before we reach the meadows and
they need to rest for it. Three days of travel have worn
them down."

With every hour Fernando seemed more like the
man who had smiled so pleasantly at Jim when they
first met. The sheepherder had almost forgotten that
he hadn't wanted Jim to come along. So far, everything
had gone well and his own anxiety was much lessened.

That evening as they sat by the fire, he talked for the
first time of his wife and little boy in the mountains
across the sea.

"When I have money enough I will send for them,"
he said. "But I must save for another year or two. If I

48

lose this job, it will be hard for me to get another. Last year, you see—"

Suddenly he stopped and scowled. He was a proud man. He hated to speak of what had happened last year.

But Jim said nothing. Only his silence was a good silence which said, "Go on if you like. I am listening."

So at last Fernando went on. "Last year all went well until late in the summer. Then a mountain lion came in the night and killed twenty-seven sheep. My gun was unloaded, and in the dark I could not find the ammunition."

He brooded for a long while, staring at the fire.

"A dog was killed, too. He was a good dog."

Later he said, "I had been hunting and came back tired. Any man might forget to reload his gun."

Jim nodded. He was beginning to understand the devil of regret and hurt pride which lived in Fernando.

The sheepherder seemed to read his thought, for he went on. "When the boss knew what had happened he was very angry. I did not deceive him. I told him what had happened just as it happened. He said I had better go back to my own land. He said that no one here

49

would hire me after that. But later on, he said that he would give me one more chance. This year, if I lose more than half a dozen sheep, it will be the end."

A little later he exclaimed in a loud voice, "I have tended sheep all my life and I am a good sheepherder! I'll show the boss! And I'll send for my wife and son! He could have trusted me. I didn't need a boy to spy on me."

"Yes, you are a good sheepherder."

"I did not mean to speak like that," Fernando said in a different voice. "I am a proud man and I have a temper. It is the boss who has not treated me right. You have been a good boy from the beginning." And he gave Jim the smile that had first made the boy like him.

Like two friends they lay down on their sheepskins under their blankets, sleeping for a few minutes and then one or another wakening to make sure that all was well with the sheep. Jim was very tired, partly from herding the flock on the trail, but more from what he had felt while passing by the Canyon of the Dead. Later the moon would rise and then the cliffs would be more terrible than ever.

But the moon did not rise and Jim sank into a deep sleep. It was the old dog who wakened him, thrusting his cold wet nose against Jim's neck.

As the boy woke up, he felt something else cold and damp lightly brushing his face.

In a moment he was wide awake, shaking Fernando by the shoulder.

"Wake up, wake up!" he shouted. "It's snowing!"

It was snowing harder and harder with every minute. In the fall it would not have mattered so much, for by then the ewes would have been protected again by their fleeces. But now, just after shearing, they could catch cold easily. Such storms usually lasted a day and a night, and that would be enough to kill perhaps half the flock.

Fernando was like a man who has been struck on the head. He was stunned. He did not even say, "It was the boss who said that it was time for the ewes to go."

"The stars were out when we went to bed," he muttered over and over again.

And all the time the snow fell more heavily.

"What are we going to do?" Jim asked.

"We can't go into the mountains," said Fernando. "We can only go down, back into the valley away from the snow. We will save some of the sheep at least."

Jim felt something against his knees. It was old Goes-Off-By-Herself, with a shadowy lamb beside her. She, for one, would never live to reach the valley. Nor would many lambs get there.

Spot whined anxiously somewhere near him. The sheep were almost silent.

Jim did not recognize his own voice. "I know where a cave is," he said. "A big cave. We will go there."

A dark late dawn found them at the beginning of the trail into the Canyon of the Dead. Even then, Jim hesitated. Wasn't it better for sheep to die than for something terrible to happen to men? He was almost relieved when the flock refused to follow the old trail along the narrow bench of rock which led across the

cliff. One side of the trail was a sheer drop down to the floor of the canyon.

The sheep huddled, bleating and crowding back. The young collie's wild, frightened barks only added to the panic, and though the old dog was grimly trying to force the sheep to the trail, they dodged back as often as he drove them toward it.

"It's no use," said Fernando at last. "It can't be done."

Jim turned away. They'd have to get back to the

valley, after all. If half the sheep must die, they must die. But, in turning, he almost stumbled over Goes-Off-By-Herself and the black lamb. Her neck and shoulders showed in the dim light, marked with streaks of black salve over the scars of the coyote's teeth. In all the panic of the sheep, she was quite calm because she was near the boy who had helped her.

"She has a better heart than I have," Jim thought, ashamed. He walked out along the narrow, snow-covered ledge, calling to the ewe to follow.

And the old sheep came, setting down her feet slowly and deliberately, looking for good footing. And after her came the black lamb.

Spot seized the opportunity. Quietly, calmly, he singled out a sheep and edged her to the trail. And suddenly she followed the black lamb and her own lamb followed her. And Spot, with Fernando's help now, chose another sheep and another until all at once the flock was following. At the head of the sheep went Jim Boy-Who-Loves-Sheep, and now he never faltered. The sheep must not crowd on that narrow path. They must come along steadily like a cord being unwound. He saw the dark low mouth of the cave looming ahead,

56

curtained in falling snow. It was curtained in snow,
but the interior was dry; the snow fell past the entrance
like the blanket in the doorway of a Navajo hogan.

Inside all was sheltered, and, without letting himself
hesitate, Jim stepped into the haunted cave. He had
almost forgotten his fear. He was thinking only of the
sheep. He sang to them:

> *"Into the house of the earth,*
> *Through the doorway of rock,*
> *Enter in peace."*

The sheep came, forming a slowly growing pool of life along the floor of the great cave. They filled it almost from wall to wall, but there was room for all, for every ewe and bleating lamb. Last of all, his eyebrows and hair thatched with snow, came Fernando, hauling the pack burro after him.

And then there was only the storm outside, and inside the animals settling down to doze away the hours ahead. Their breath soon warmed the cave, and Fernando, at its entrance, lighted a small fire from odds and ends of the sticks he found there.

"We'll sit here where the path begins," he said. "Nothing can come in or out. Now for the coffee we didn't have this morning! And a can of peaches in celebration. By tomorrow this storm will have blown out and we can go on to the summer pasture. Heaven be praised, the sheep weren't out in the storm long enough to get cold or tired."

Jim nodded without speaking. He thought that there were many unseen beings in the cave whom the breath of the flock and the flames of a fire could not warm. But if ghosts were there, they gave no sign. Perhaps, thought the boy, they too love the sheep and the lambs.

60

They have opened the door of their hogan for us. Under his breath he thanked them, calling them "Grand-fathers" out of respect. Everything was all right. Spot was asleep beside the fire. The burro stood with drooping head, half asleep too. The flock was at peace. The storm which they had felt in the air had come and they had escaped its dangers. It was unseasonable and it would be the last. Now only summer and the summer pasture lay ahead.

"Coffee's ready," said Fernando. "This snow will be good for the grass. The storm will be gone by morning."

They ate and drank in silence, enjoying themselves.

Only when they had finished did Fernando give a low laugh.

"To think that I was angry because you came with me!" he said. "How little one knows what is good and what is bad! It wasn't that I didn't like you."

There was no need for Jim to answer. He got out the salve and dressed Goes-Off-By-Herself's wounds. They were healing well.

"What ewe will you take?" Fernando asked from behind the smoke of his cigarette. "There's a good one over there, with two strong lambs."

But Jim shook his head, looking up from his work.

"I shall take this one," he said.

"But she's old, and injured, and has only one lamb," Fernando protested.

"She has the heart of a warrior," said Jim.